IN MY TREEHOUSE

IN MY TREEHOUSE

story by Alice Schertle
pictures by Meredith Dunham

Lothrop, Lee & Shepard Books
New York

 Inquiries should be addressed to Lothrop, Lee & Shepard Books, a division of William Morrow & Company, Inc., 105 Madison Avenue, New York, New York 10016. Printed in the United States of America. First Edition.
1 2 3 4 5 6 7 8 9 10

Library of Congress Cataloging in Publication Data. Schertle, Alice. In my treehouse. Summary: A child describes the pleasures offered by a tree house and the real and imaginary adventures to be enjoyed in one. [1. Tree houses--Fiction] I. Dunham, Meredith, ill. II. Title. PZ7.S3442In 1983 [E] 82-10016
ISBN 0-688-01638-3 ISBN 0-688-01639-1 (lib. bdg.) AACR2

To John, who lets me visit his treehouse
—A.S.
To Jamie
—M.D.

When I'm up high in my treehouse I'm all alone. Just me, myself, and I. On the crook of a nearby branch, a place just right for a bird nest, I hung a shoelace, some string, a piece of rag, and some of my hair. But no bird has made a nest here yet. Sometimes I wonder if the birds think I'm another bird. Maybe they think that my treehouse is a giant nest, and one nest in this tree is enough.

When I'm in my treehouse I think about things. I think about riding a roller coaster, about a dream I had, about being the strongest person in the world, and about being invisible. I think about flying an airplane, taming a lion, and having an elephant for a pet.

Sometimes I think about lunch. Then I climb down my ladder and go get two bananas. I put them inside my backpack. I might put a piece of cheese in, too. And some gingersnaps, if there are any.

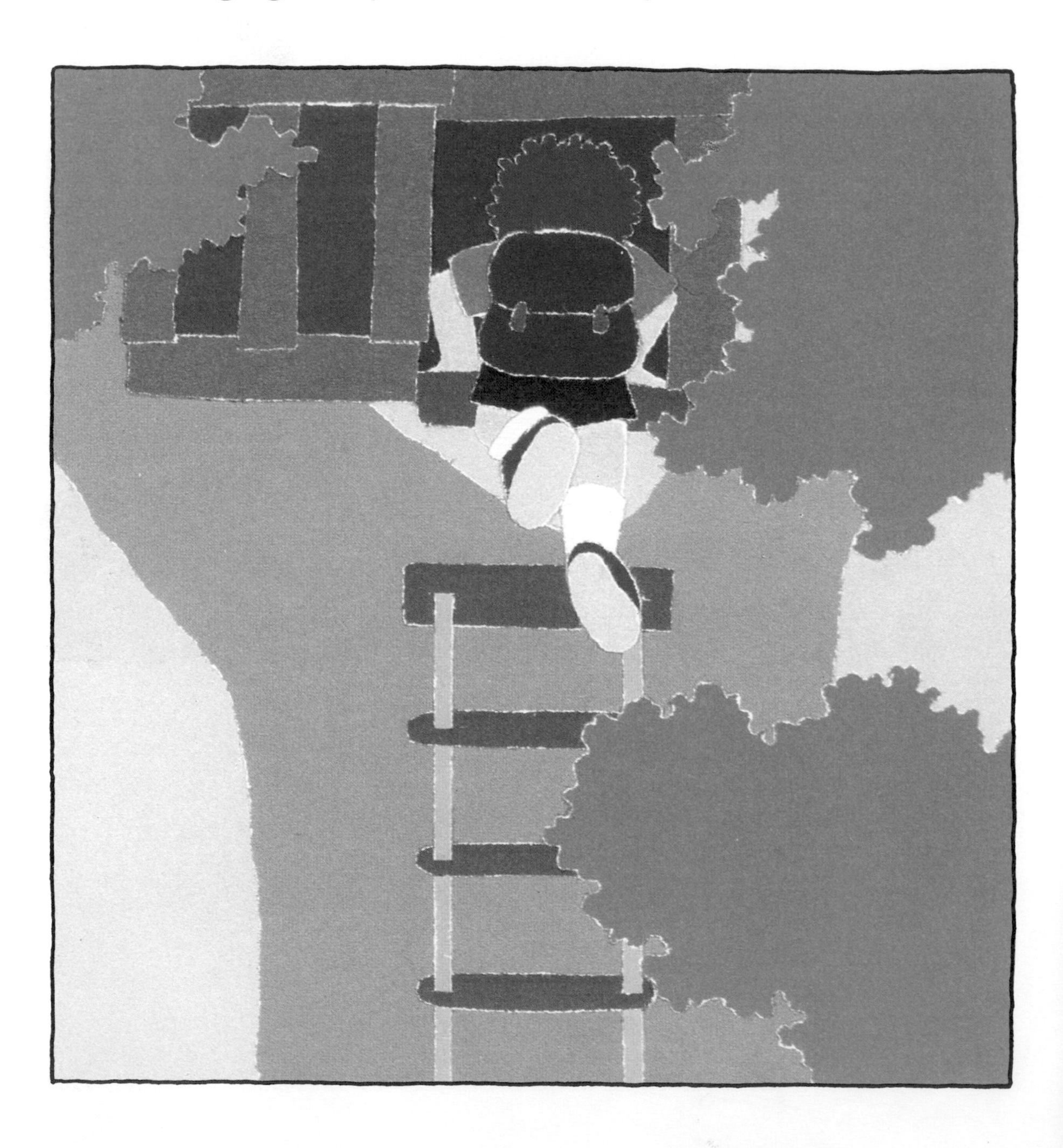

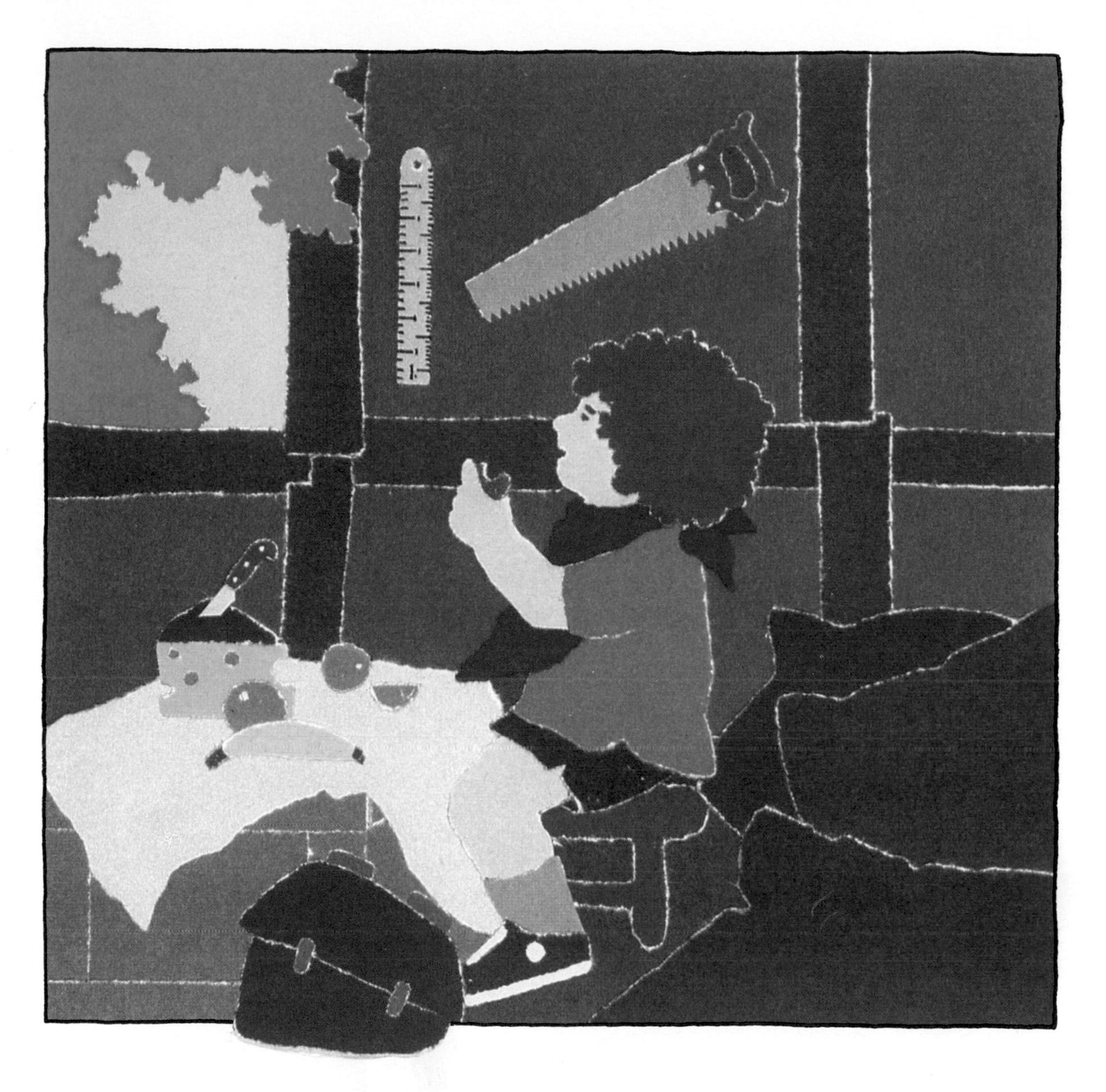

When I'm back in my treehouse, I pretend I'm an explorer, alone in the woods, and that the food in my pack has to last a whole month. I just nibble on a little of everything, and put the rest away. Then I pretend a whole month has gone by. So I open my pack again and eat all that's left of my lunch.

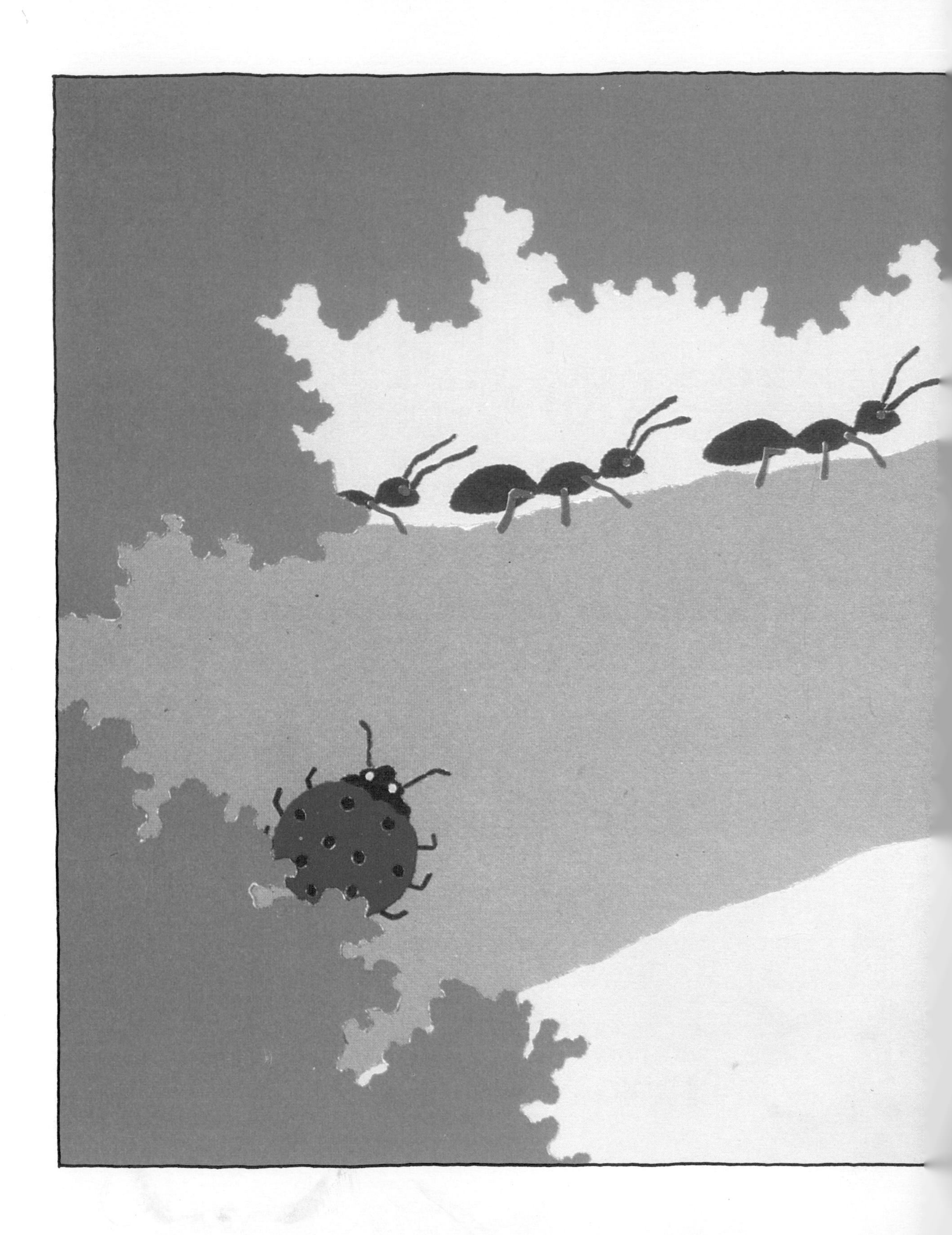

Ants like my lunch and my treehouse, too. Crawling up the trunk of my tree, they make a long black line that disappears into a little crack on a branch. I like to think there's a whole ant city in my treehouse tree, with ant streets and ant stores, and little ant houses. So they'll think I'm a good neighbor, I put a gingersnap crumb out on their branch. It's a whole huge cake for my treehouse ants.

Tied to my treehouse is a rope with a bucket on one end. If I lower the bucket to the ground, anyone who passes by can leave a message. Once when I pulled my bucket mailbox up, a note inside said, “Dinner’s ready.”

A bucket on a rope can be an elevator, too. I caught a woolly bear and put it in my bucket. “Going up, Mr. Caterpillar!” I said. Then, “Top floor, everyone out.”

Dinner is ready

I tried to give my cat a ride, but when I started to pull up the bucket, she jumped right out. Cats don't need elevator buckets, I decided. They don't need ladders, either. My cat can climb into my treehouse twice as fast as I can. If I call her she usually pretends she doesn't hear. But when she's ready, she'll be up in a flash to see what I'm doing.

On sunny days, I might haul a bucket of books into my treehouse. I make a nice, soft corner with an old, bunched-up bedspread. I sink down into it and read. Just me, myself, and I. And a hundred books or so.

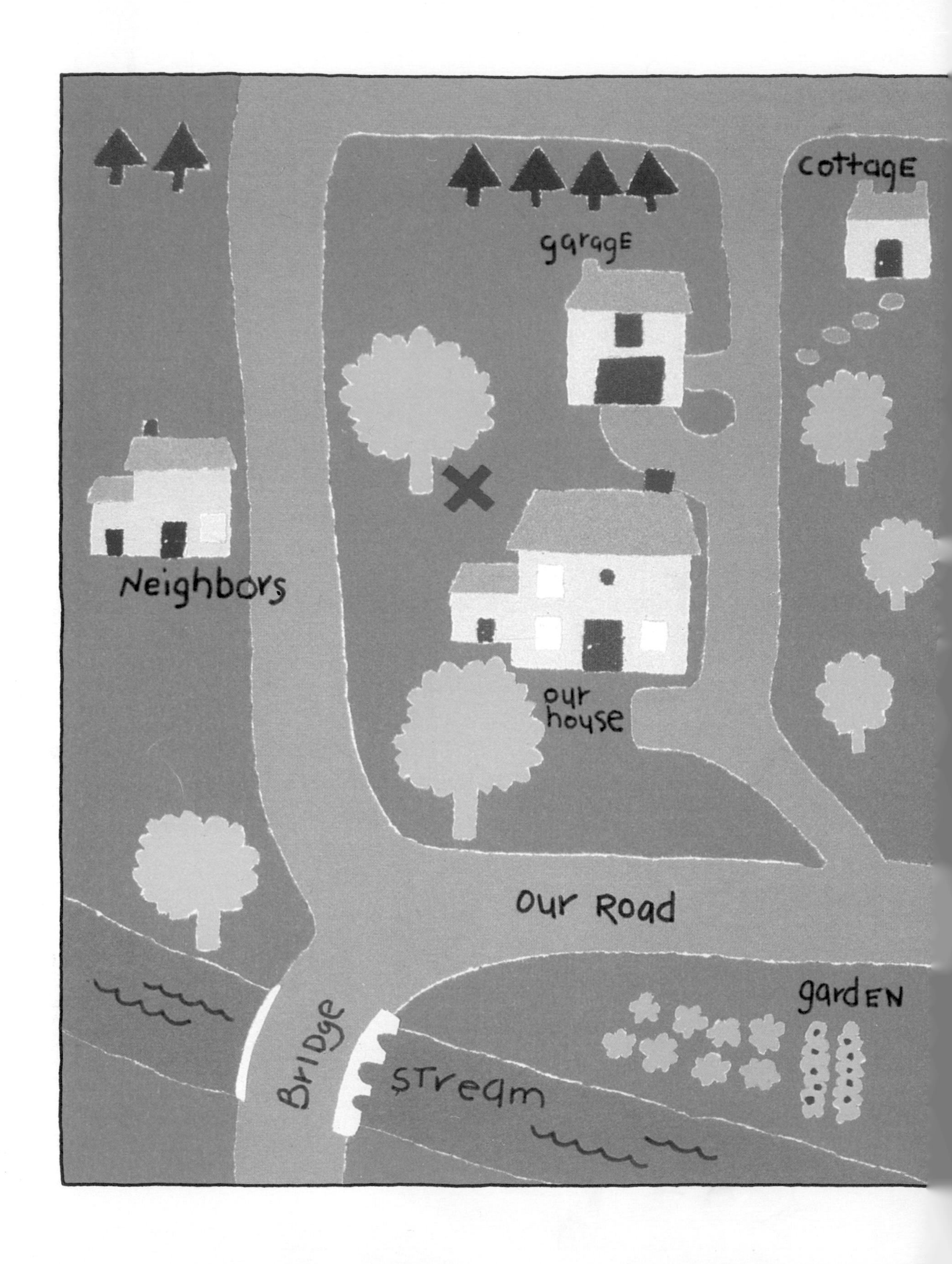
cottage
garage
Neighbors
our house
Our Road
garden
Bridge
stream

From up in my treehouse, I can see my whole yard. I can see my neighbors' yards, too. I have a map of my neighborhood that I made in my treehouse. X marks the spot where the treasure is buried.

I know what the treasure is. It's twenty-two pennies that have been scrubbed with a toothbrush until they look like gold. They're wrapped inside a sock that's inside a jelly jar that's right underneath my treehouse tree. I buried it there. It's a secret no one knows, except me, myself, and I.

My treasure is safe when I'm in my treehouse tower. I can look out and spot enemies coming from miles away. When I see them, I sound the alarm. "Bong! Bong!" I clang my bucket. "Take cover! Take cover!"

Once I spent all night in my treehouse. I used our old brown sleeping bag that smells like the garage. I found out that lots of things make noises at night, and it's too

dark to see what's out there. So I was glad when my cat came up to sleep with me. Her purr is so loud you can hardly hear anything else.

In the morning I had four mosquito bites. My mom sent orange juice and muffins up in my delivery bucket. I shared the muffins with my cat. The treehouse ants shared, too.

I ate my breakfast at the table and bench I made from scraps of wood. I keep a hammer and a can of nails in my treehouse in case I have to make repairs. And when I want to move the furniture, I just pry it up and build it somewhere else.

I love being up high when it's windy. The branches whip back and forth, and leaves blow all around me. Even the big old tree trunk starts to sway. Sometimes it feels like my whole treehouse is going to fly off with the wind. I hammer a few extra nails in, just in case.

In my treehouse I can lie on my back and look up through leaves. I can listen to birds and watch the ants. I can guard my treasure and I can curl up and read. I can do all these things in my treehouse. Just me, myself, and I.

Alice Schertle's fourth book for Lothrop followed considerable time spent observing her son John and sitting in his backyard retreat. "I can promise you," she wrote, "the ants part is true." A native of Los Angeles, California, Ms. Schertle attended the University of Southern California, from which she received a Bachelor of Science degree in the field of education. She brings to her many books for children, including Lothrop's *The Gorilla in the Hall*, *The April Fool*, and *Hob Goblin and the Skeleton*, the wisdom of a former teacher and volunteer librarian, the insights of a mother of three, and the enthusiasm of a children's book collector. Ms. Schertle and her family live on the outskirts of Los Angeles in a half-century-old house on one and a half acres, which they share with an ever-changing number of animals.

Meredith Dunham was born in Brownsville, Texas, and graduated from the University of Texas in Austin with a Bachelor of Fine Arts degree in art history. Since then, she has held a variety of jobs in Washington, D.C., and New York City while pursuing her illustration career. Although her work has appeared in numerous books and magazines and has been exhibited in a one-woman show, *In My Treehouse* is her picture-book première.